saviour pirotta

Firebird

paintings by

catherine hyde

templar books

an imprint of Candlewick Press

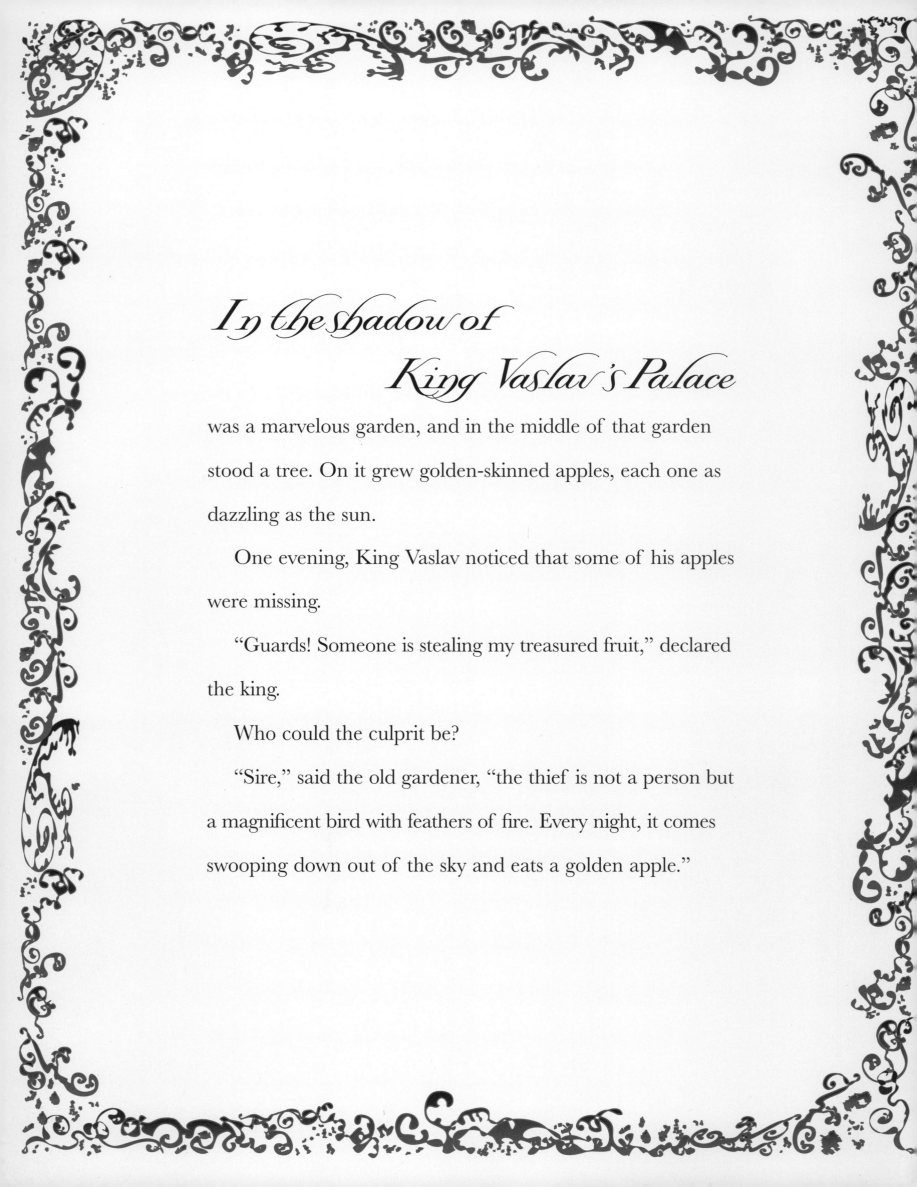

In the shadow of
King Vaslav's Palace

was a marvelous garden, and in the middle of that garden

stood a tree. On it grew golden-skinned apples, each one as

dazzling as the sun.

One evening, King Vaslav noticed that some of his apples

were missing.

"Guards! Someone is stealing my treasured fruit," declared

the king.

Who could the culprit be?

"Sire," said the old gardener, "the thief is not a person but

a magnificent bird with feathers of fire. Every night, it comes

swooping down out of the sky and eats a golden apple."

"A firebird?" said the king's two elder sons, Dimitri and Vasili, with a laugh. "Do you still believe in fairy tales, old man, or are you trying to make fools of us all?"

"I want the thief caught, be it bird, animal, or man," said the king. "Whoever brings the thief to me shall win a quarter of my kingdom."

A quarter of the kingdom? Prince Dimitri was determined to win such a valuable prize. That night he camped out under the apple tree, his sword across his lap. Come morning, however, he woke up to discover that the thief had struck while he'd been asleep.

The next night, Prince Vasili offered to guard the tree. But, as he was also used to an easy life in the palace, he too fell asleep, and the thief stole another of the golden-skinned apples.

In the evening the king's third son, Prince Ivan, said, "Papa, tonight it is my turn to try to catch the robber."

Now, everyone in the palace considered Ivan to be young and foolish.

"Why would you succeed where your brothers failed?" said the king. "Do not waste my time."

he too fell asleep

swooped down from the sky

But that night Prince Ivan hid behind a bush close to the apple tree. He took a flask of water with him, and every time he felt sleepy, he splashed cold water on his face.

Shortly after midnight, a rosy light shone over the garden, as if the sun were coming up. Then, just as the old gardener had said, a great bird with feathers that seemed to be made of fire swooped down from the sky, settled on the apple tree, and started to peck at an apple.

Anyone else would simply have gaped in wonder. Not Ivan! Quick as a hare, he darted out from behind the bush and grabbed the firebird by her tail. The creature shrieked and beat her enormous wings to break free. Her flapping wings looked like a thousand sparklers, blazing together on Festival Night, but Ivan did not let go.

He held on until he heard a snap. The firebird had broken free and soared up into the sky, leaving only a single golden feather in Ivan's hand.

When Ivan showed the feather to his father, it lit up the entire throne room.

"So, the legend is true!" declared the king. "He who brings me the firebird will inherit half my kingdom."

Right away, Prince Dimitri set out to find the firebird. He rode on and on until he came to a crossroads at the edge of the kingdom. There he saw a huge rock on which was carved a warning:

Take the middle road, and you will suffer hunger and cold.
Take the right road, and you will live, though your horse will die.
Take the left road, and you will die, though your horse will live.

"They all sound too dangerous," said Prince Dimitri, used to the sheltered life of a prince, and he galloped back to the palace.

The next day, Prince Vasili set out to catch the firebird. Not having any of his advisers to do the thinking for him, he couldn't decide which path was best and returned home to his father.

Then Prince Ivan said to the king, "Papa, may I go in search of the firebird too?"

"Why should you succeed where your older brothers have failed?" said King Vaslav. "Do not bother me, Ivan."

one feather

But Ivan saddled an old horse and rode out into the night. At the edge of the kingdom, he came to the boulder and read the warning.

I don't like being cold and hungry, thought Ivan, *so the middle road is not for me. And I don't want to die, so the road on the left is no good, either. There is no other way but to risk the road on the right.*

He'd hardly galloped past the boulder when he found himself in a dark and gloomy forest. He heard a growl, and a gray wolf, huge as a lion, leaped into his path. It knocked Ivan off the old horse, which it gobbled up in one mouthful.

"You are a brave lad," said Gray Wolf. "Anyone else would have turned around at the boulder. Climb onto my back, and I will take you wherever you want to go."

"Take me to the firebird," ordered Prince Ivan, clambering onto Gray Wolf's back.

Away they sped, out of the gloomy forest and into a city. Gray Wolf stopped near a high wall, overgrown with ivy.

"On the other side of this wall is the garden of King Dolmat," said the wolf. "In the summer house you'll find three birds in dazzling gold cages—the third holds the firebird. Take the firebird as she sleeps, but I warn you: leave the cage behind."

Ivan stole into the garden and found the three birds in the summer house just as the wolf had described. He was about to put his hand inside the cage when he noticed it was made of pure gold. Surely it would be a pity to leave such a treasure behind. He tried lifting it off its hook, but immediately alarm bells rang all over the palace and he was captured by the king's guards.

"I see by your fine clothes that you are a prince," said King Dolmat. "Why would you try to steal my firebird?"

"It is your bird that is the thief," replied Ivan. "It took my father's golden apples, and I was sent to bring it to justice."

"I should lock you up in prison," said King Dolmat, "but instead I shall send you on a mission for me. Beyond the mountains to the west lives King Afron. He promised me a horse with a golden mane but never sent it. Bring me the horse, and I'll give you the firebird and her cage."

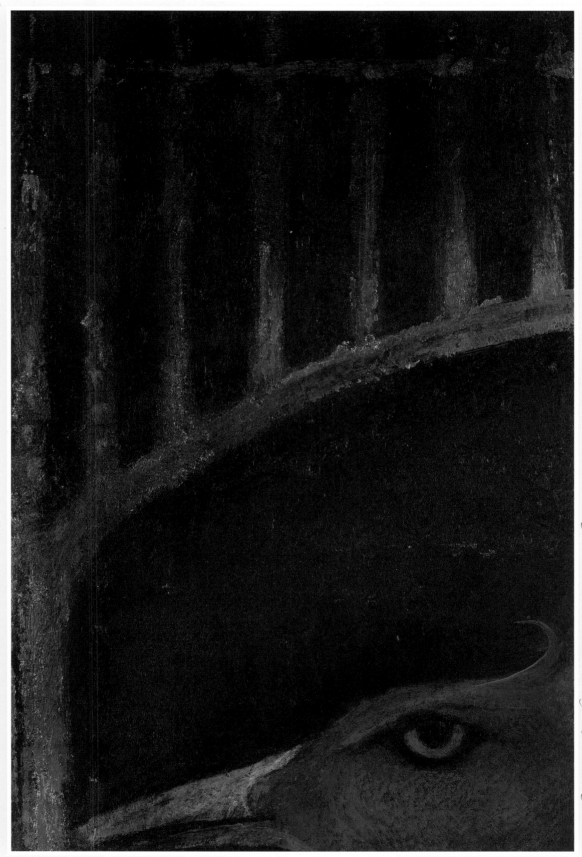

its cage was made of pure gold

So Ivan returned to the wolf and said, "Gray Wolf, take me to the horse with the golden mane."

Swifter than the wind, Gray Wolf carried Ivan out of the kingdom and beyond the mountains. There he came to a wall overgrown with roses.

"Behind this wall are King Afron's stables," said Gray Wolf. "Inside you'll find three horses. One of them is the mare with the golden mane, who will be asleep. Lead her out by her halter and she will not awake. But I warn you, Prince Ivan: do not touch her bridle."

swifter than the wind

Ivan crept into the stables. He was leading the horse out by its halter when he noticed that the bridle was covered in diamonds. Surely he could not leave so great a prize behind. But as he lifted the bridle from its hook on the wall, alarms sounded, and once again Ivan was caught.

"I should send you to the gallows," said King Afron. "But I see by your soft hands that you are a man of noble blood, so instead I will ask you to do me a small favor. Beyond the river to the east lies the country of King Saltan. He promised to let me marry his beautiful daughter, Princess Helen, but now he refuses to send her. Bring me the princess, and I will give you the horse and its bridle."

Once again, Prince Ivan returned to Gray Wolf and they galloped out of King Afron's country and across the mighty river until they reached King Saltan's realm. There Gray Wolf stopped near a wall that was overgrown with pomegranates.

"Behind this wall sits Princess Helen, asleep with her book," said Gray Wolf. "Lead her out by the hand, and she will not wake. But on no account are you to touch the book."

Prince Ivan was about to scale the wall when the wolf stopped him.

"Ivan, since you took no notice of my warnings about the birdcage or the bridle, I know you will not obey me this time, either. Go back along the road and wait for me there."

Prince Ivan waited, and at sundown Gray Wolf returned with the sleeping princess held gently in his mouth. He set her down on the grass, and she opened her eyes.

"Don't be afraid," said Prince Ivan. "I've come to take you to your bridegroom."

she opened her eyes

The two of them had barely climbed onto Gray Wolf's back, however, when they heard the blast of trumpets. Helen's maid had seen the wolf and raised the alarm. But no guard on horseback could outrun Gray Wolf, and soon he was crossing the river into King Afron's country.

"Ivan, I don't love King Afron," whispered Princess Helen as they approached the palace.

"Whom do you love, then?" asked Prince Ivan.

"I love you, Ivan, and I believe you love me, too," replied Princess Helen.

Together the prince and princess turned to Gray Wolf. "Will you help us?" asked Ivan.

crossing the river

"I have already helped you more than enough, Prince Ivan," said Gray Wolf. "But we have grown to be friends, so I shall do what I can. Just promise me that the next time you see the full moon, you will call out my name!"

Gray Wolf patted the damp earth with his paw and in an instant turned into a young woman who was the spitting image of Princess Helen.

Ivan presented him to King Afron, who had no reason to suspect trickery. Claiming the horse with the golden mane, he then galloped back to the real Princess Helen, who had been hiding outside the palace.

the ring

It had grown dark, and Prince Ivan and Princess Helen were well on their way to King Dolmat's castle when Ivan looked up at the moon and suddenly remembered the wolf.

"Gray Wolf! Gray Wolf!" he cried.

At his palace, King Afron was about to put a wedding ring on his bride's finger when—in a flash—she turned back into a snarling wolf and leaped over the palace wall. The king called for his guards, but no armed guard was a match for Gray Wolf. In no time at all, the wolf met up with Ivan and Helen near King Dolmat's palace.

Outside the palace, Ivan said to Gray Wolf, "Princess Helen does not want to part with the mare. Can you help us again?"

"Yes," replied Gray Wolf, "but Ivan, do not forget to call my name again the next time you see the moon."

He changed himself into a horse exactly like the mare with the golden mane, and Ivan left him with King Dolmat in return for the firebird in its golden cage.

Later that night, while King Dolmat was riding near his castle, Ivan saw the full moon and called out, "Gray Wolf! Gray Wolf!" Instantly the king's horse changed into a wolf that leaped away into the forest.

he changed himself into a horse

King Dolmat summoned his guard, but what soldier can find a wolf in a dark forest? In no time at all, the three friends had met up once more.

When they came to the boulder at the crossroads, Gray Wolf said, "I fear the time has come for us to part."

Ivan and Helen both hugged Gray Wolf, who then slipped away into the shadows, never to be seen again.

That evening, King Vaslav welcomed them home with open arms. As a wedding present, he gave Ivan half of his kingdom, as well as the glorious firebird and her cage.

no bird likes to live in a cage

But Prince Ivan decided to set the firebird free,

for no one likes

to live in a cage,

and it feasted on the golden-skinned apples

for the rest of her days.

The Story of the Firebird

The image of the bird of fire appears in the folktales of many countries. The Ancient Egyptians believed in a holy bird called the Bennu, said to be the soul of the sun-god Ra. It was sometimes depicted as a golden eagle with golden and red feathers. The Bennu was responsible for the Nile floods that brought prosperity to Egypt. The Ancient Greeks, Phoenicians, and Persians also had similar myths. The most popular stories about the firebird today come from Eastern Europe and Russia. Here the magical creature is often portrayed as a peacock with eyes in its golden feathers. In some versions, pearls fall from its beak every time it caws, and its song brings a good harvest to the farmers.

The firebird in these tales is often the source of good fortune. But finding one of its glowing feathers forces the hero of the story to set off on a difficult quest, usually to capture the fabled creature at the behest of a king or father.

Many writers and artists have been inspired by stories about the firebird. Perhaps the most well known is Igor Stravinsky's music for the Russian ballet, The Firebird. First performed by the world-famous Ballet Russes in 1910, the story weaves together ideas from different versions of the tale of the firebird. Like the bird's feather, which can light up a whole room, this ballet is still holding audiences spellbound even a hundred years later!

the

✽treasured fruit ✽he too fell asleep

✽one feather ✽the edge of the kingdom

✽its cage was made of pure gold

✽leading the horse ✽Princess

✽crossing the river ✽the horse

✽the ring ✽he changed himself

✽no bird likes to live in a cage

paintings

wooped down from the sky

❀out of the gloomy forest

❀swifter than the wind

Helen   ❀she opened her eyes

with the golden mane

nto a horse   ❀a wedding

❀the golden-skinned apple

For Jode Hartley Paton.
S. P.

For my brother, Julius.
C. H.

Text copyright © 2010 by Saviour Pirotta
Illustrations copyright © 2010 by Catherine Hyde

First U.S. edition 2010

Library of Congress Cataloging-in-Publication Data pending.
ISBN 978-0-7636-5076-6

10 11 12 13 14 15 16 CCP 10 9 8 7 6 5 4 3 2 1

Printed in Shenzhen, Guangdong, China

This book was typeset in Baskerville. The illustrations were done in acrylic on paper with gold and copper leaf.

Edited by Libby Hamilton • Designed by Janie Louise Hunt

TEMPLAR BOOKS
an imprint of
Candlewick Press
99 Dover Street
Somerville, Massachusetts 02144
www.candlewick.com

For L. B. Love you always.

For R. T. Thank you.
J. L. H.